Chubby Roars the Loudest Roar

written by

Betty Misheiker

illustrated by

Ilona Suschitkzky

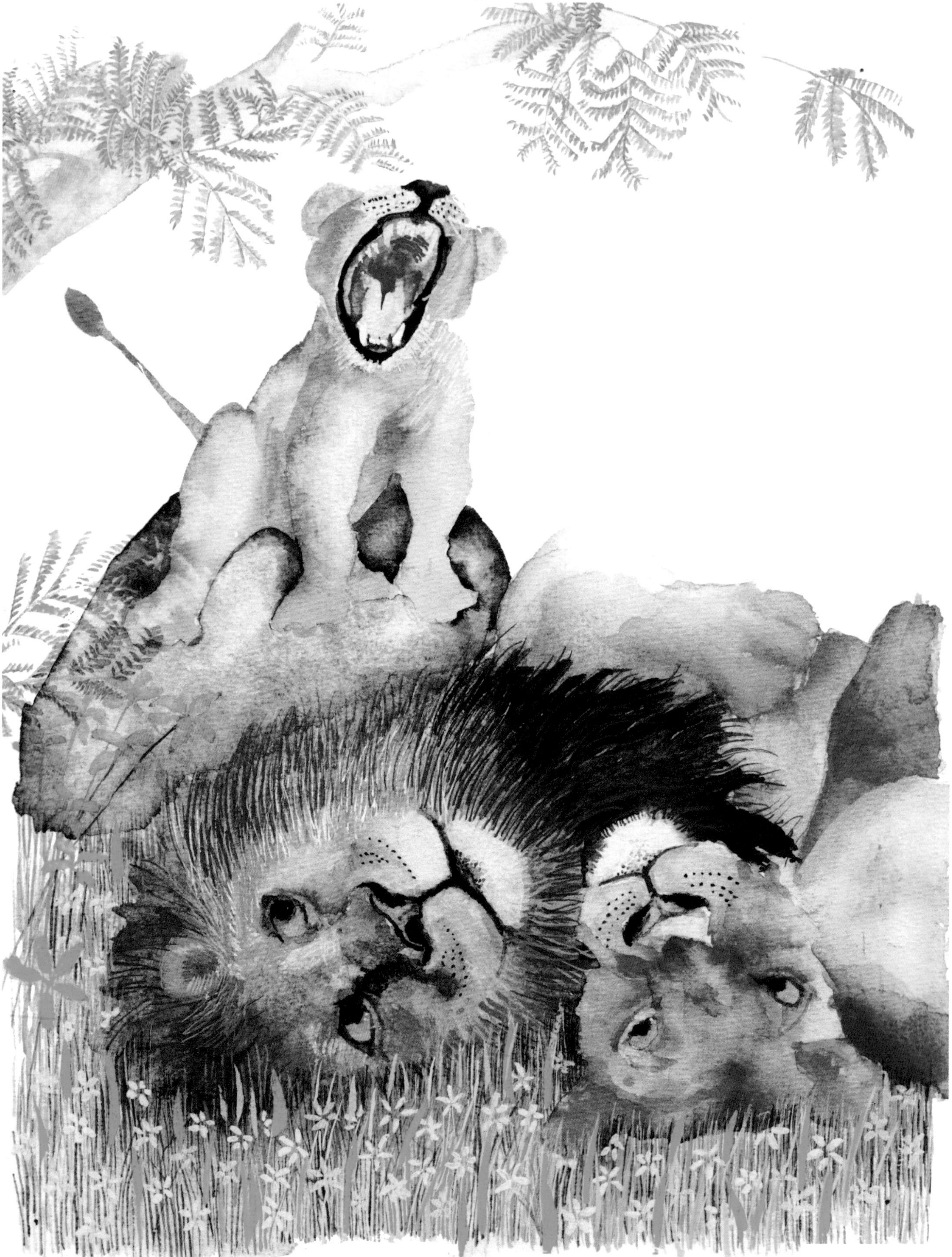

"Grrruhm-gruhm!" growled Chubby the lion cub as fiercely as he could, "grrrruhm-gruhm-grrrrruhm!" "No-no, not good enough, Chubby, no!" said Mama Lion, "That's not one bit frightening! Try again, louder! Much louder!"

"Grrrrrrrrrr-uhm!" growled Chubby, trying his best to squeeze out a big roar, but his mother still shook her head.

She turned to Chubby's Papa who lay dozing in the shade of a tree nearby. "I don't think Chubby will ever learn to roar like a real lion," she said, "unless you start showing him how!"

Chubby's Papa sighed, raised his fierce-looking, shaggy head, blinked his yellow eyes, twitched the tip of his tail and gave a grumbling-rumbling ROAR-R-R-R-R-R-R that made the earth tremble and sent everybody in the bush for miles around scampering for their lives! Papa lion yawned, stretched his legs, rested his nose on his paws and closed his eyes.

"Wow!" said Chubby, "Wow!"

"See?" said his Mama, "That is a roar! Now you try!"

"I don't want to!" said Chubby.

"You must," said Mama Lion, "You have to learn!"

"Why have I got to learn things all the time?" Chubby grumbled. "All the time! All the time! How to roar! How to creep and stalk through the grass, and how to spring out suddenly, and how to chase away flies from my nose, and what I can eat and what I can't eat and all sorts of things like that! Why?"

"Because you're growing up," said his Mama, "That's why Chubby! A lion who can't roar properly is a positive disgrace! You wouldn't want everybody to laugh at you, would you?"

"Grrr-ow-uhm!" muttered Chubby, "I don't care!"

"Yes you DO care!" said Mama Lion rolling over onto her side in the soft grass under the tree, "of course you do! But now we want to rest, so off with you! Practise your roar, and don't go too far away!"

Overhead the sun blazed down hot and yellow as
Chubby trotted away across the veld. A slight breeze
stirred the long grass and a wild bee buzzed about
looking for pollen. Somewhere high up, on the tip
of a tree a little bird chirped twee-twee-twee, quickly
like that, and again twee-twee-twee! And far, far off
across the river Chubby could hear the pack of
Chacma baboons who lived there, grunting and
calling to each other, saying, "Uhu-uhu-uhu!
Yukkoo-yukkoo-yukkoo! Uhu! Yukkoo-yukkoo!"

Suddenly Chubby stopped and peered through
the clumps of grass. In the middle of a small
clearing he could see Wally the baby warthog
kneeling down on his two front knees, sniffling
and snuffling and digging away in the ground
with his nose.

"What are you doing, Wally?" asked Chubby
coming closer.

"I'm digging for roots of course!" said Wally,
"can't you see?" Crunch-crunch, went Wally's
teeth. "Yummy-yum-yum! That was a delicious
one! So crisp and spicy!"
"Are roots nice Wally?" asked Chubby suddenly
starting to feel very hungry.

"Of course!" mumbled Wally, "Roots are delicious! The most delicious thing in the whole world! Except maybe for little green shoots! They're nice too – and bulbs! I get lots of ordinary things to eat every day, like grass and leaves, but roots are the yummy-yummiest treat because they're so spicy!"

"What's spicy?" Chubby asked.

Wally stopped munching and looked at Chubby. "Here, taste some and you'll see" he said.

Chubby licked his lips. I – I think I had better go and ask my Mama first!" He turned around and ran back as quickly as he could.

"Mama! Mama!" called Chubby.

Mama Lion jumped up in alarm. "What is it, Chubby?"

"Wally the warthog is digging up roots!" said Chubby.
"He wants to give me some to taste! Is that all right,
Mama?"
"What!" cried Chubby's mother, opening her eyes wide,
"A lion eat roots? The very idea! You certainly may NOT!
It would RUIN your digestion!"
"Oh, please Mama" pleaded Chubby, "Wally says roots are
delicious."
"NO Chubby!"
" - and spicy, Mama, I've never tasted spicy!"
"NO! Chubby! Roots may be delicious for warthogs to
eat, but not for us! Spicy indeed! MEAT is what lions eat
Chubby! Meat gives us strength to roar!"
"Only a taste Mama?"

"No, Chubby!"

"Just this once?" pleaded Chubby.

"No, no, no!" said Chubby's mother, "Now off with you!"
Chubby stamped away very cross indeed. "I will! I will!
I will!" he muttered to himself, "I WILL. I want to taste
spicy!"

By the time Chubby got back to the clearing in the grass,
Wally had disappeared but there was still a little piece of
something that looked like a root lying on the ground.
Chubby put it in his mouth and began to chew. At first it
tasted like nothing, then a strange, peppery sort of feeling
spread along his tongue and down his throat and up into
his nose, burning like fire and making tears run out of his
eyes.

"Yeeeeee-uuuuuuggghhh!" cried Chubby, quickly spitting out
as much as he could. "yugh-yugh-yugh! Ooooh! Yeeugh!
Bitter, bitter! Horrible! Horrible! Yeugh!" Chubby coughed,
sneezed, jumped around, rolled over and over on the ground
and rubbed his nose on the clumps of grass to get rid of the
horrible taste.

It took quite a while for the awful, peppery juice of the root to stop burning his throat, tickling his nose and making tears run out of his eyes.

"I'll never eat spicy again! Poof and phooey!" Chubby promised himself and sat down in the shade of some acacia trees to rest.

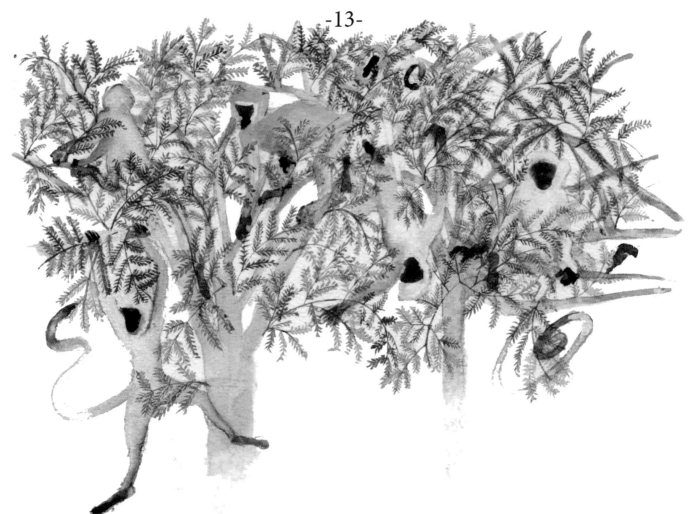

It was so peaceful there, in the quiet cool shade, that Chubby almost fell asleep. But a whole pack of little Vervet Monkeys suddenly arrived and began jumping around amongst the trees. The monkeys chattered and chattered as they played, bouncing about on the branches of the trees, chasing each other up and down the tree-trunks,

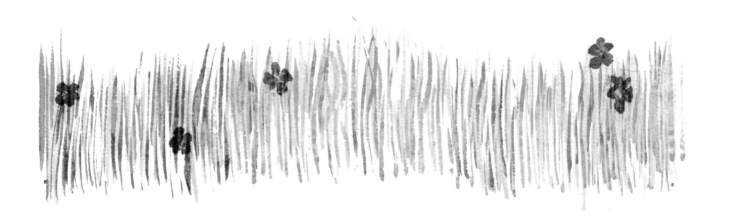

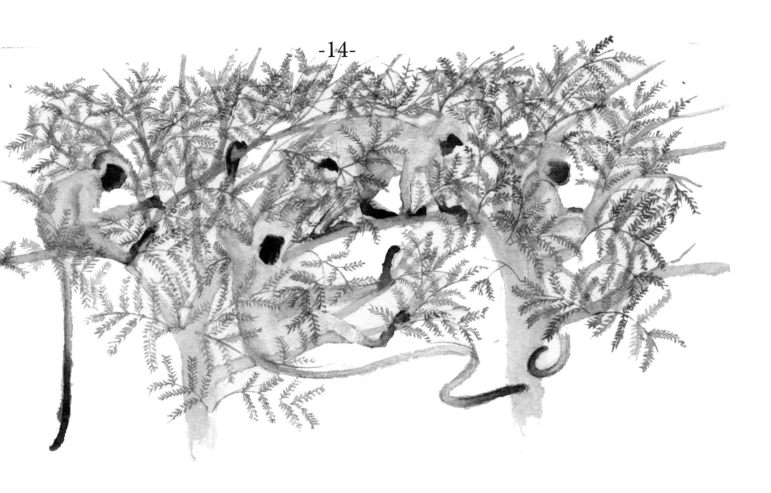

rolling over and over on the ground, racing up the trees
again, leaping from one branch to another, swinging by their
tails and flying through the air. Oh it did really look such fun!
Chubby quickly ran back to his mother.
"Mama! Mama! Mama!" he called, quite out of breath.

"What's all the noise about?" grumbled Papa Lion, twitching his whiskers and resting one of his large paws across his nose.

"What is it, Chubby?" asked his Mother.

"I've just seen monkeys swinging on the trees…" said Chubby. "They're jumping up and down and all around and hanging by their tails!"

"So…?" said Mama Lion.

"So…so could I….? Just this once…?"

"Could you what? Chubby?"

"Climb up into the trees and swing by my tail? Please… please…PLEASE!" begged Chubby.

Papa Lion gave a kind of gurgling sort of chuckling snort and turned over onto his other side.

"I don't believe my ears!" cried Mama Lion, "You want to swing in the trees like monkeys and baboons?"

"Yes! May I Mama?"

"Most certainly NOT!" said his Mama. "Lion's tails are not monkey's tails, Chubby! Monkey's legs and arms are not the same as ours! Don't you know that? Our family do not swing in trees!" and his Mama sighed and shook her head. "Really! I don't know what will become of you! If you don't look out, you're going to land in a circus or a zoo, Chubby, mark my words!"

"Well I don't care if I do!" growled Chubby walking away as sulky as can be. "I don't care if I do land in a circus or a zoo! I'm GOING to swing in the branches. If the monkeys can climb in trees and jump about and swing by their tails, why can't I? A tail is a tail is a tail, isn't it?"

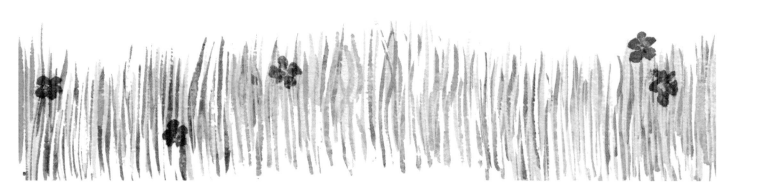

Chubby marched right back to the group of Acacia trees. He dug his litle claws into the bark of the trees and began to climb. Clinging with all his might to the smooth trunk of the tree, Chubby managed, little by little, to creep higher and still higher. But when Chubby stopped to look down over his shoulder, he nearly dropped with fright! Oooh! The ground seemed very, very far away! For a while Chubby clung there, afraid to climb higher and not at all sure what to do next.

Way up near the top of the tree the little Vervet monkeys sat peering down at him through the leaves. Unable to hold on any longer, Chubby threw himself to one side the way he had seen the monkeys do, and tried to catch hold of the nearest branch.

Of course his small paws couldn't curl around to grip the branch the way a monkey's hand can and as for his tail – it simply refused to help him in any way! Down dropped Chubby, landing on the ground with a hard thump!

"Chitter-chitter-chitter-chatter!" said the Vervet monkeys and began leaping around madly as if to show him how it should be done.

The fall was jolly sore, but Chubby picked himself up, shook each of his paws separately, and trying not to limp, walked slowly down the hillside, towards the river.

Near the water's edge, in a shallow pool of muddy water, stood Mafuta the baby hippopotamus.
"Hello Chubby!" said Mafuta in the friendliest way, "Aren't you feeling hot in your fur coat, Chubby?"
"Yes I am!" said Chubby.

"Well then come along into the water," said Mafuta, "It's lovely and cool inside all this soft, wet mud. Come on Chubby! If you like we can make some mud-pies! Would you like to make some mud pies?"

"Oh yes! I would!" cried Chubby starting to bounce up and down with excitement. "I would! I would!"

"Well, come on in then," said Mafuta. "I'll show you how to make mud pies. Look, you take a lump of this nice mishy-mushy mud and then you squash it and s-q-u-a-s-h it like this… come on Chubby!"

Chubby was about to jump into the muddy pool when he stopped.

I-I had better go and ask my Mama first," he said. "Don't go away Mafuta, I'll be right back!"

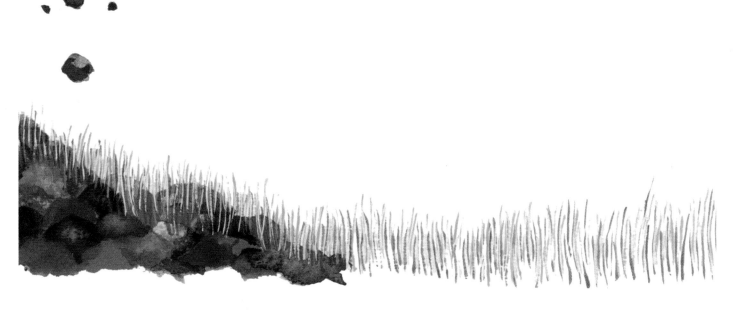

"Mama! Mama!" he called. "Mama! Mama!"

"Oh really, Chubby, you are very naughty this afternoon," his mother said. "Why do you keep disturbing us every few minutes like this? What is it now?"

"Mafuta is standing in the hippo-pool" said Chubby, "and he says it's cool and I should come inside! And you know what, Mama? He's squashing up mud for mud-pies! Can I go into the pool and make mud-pies with Mafuta? Just this once, Mama?"

Mama Lion picked Chubby up by the scruff of his neck, gave him a good shake, put him down right in front of her and waggled a paw before his nose. "How many times must I tell you, Chubby, that lions only go into water when they absolutely HAVE to! Only when it is a matter of life or death! They certainly NEVER play in the mud! Lions are the king of the beasts, Chubby, so you must learn to behave properly!

Now run along and the next time you come back we want
to hear a big, loud, ROAR! Do you understand?"
In reply, Chubby howled and growled and rolled over and
over in the grass and kicked his legs and stamped and
wished he could DO or SAY something terrible!
"I'm never, never, never, never, EVER going to roar for you
again!" he shouted as loudly as he could. "And I'm not
going to eat anymore! Or drink! Or stalk! Or spring!
Or do anything you want me to do! I don't WANT to be
king of the beasts, so there! I don't want to be a lion because
lions can't DO anything!"
Without even bothering to open his eyes, Papa Lion gave a
long, rumbling, warning roar for Chubby's benefit. "Lions
have to roar, Chubby," he growled, "And the sooner you
learn to do so, the better! So off you go and practise!"
Mumbling and grumbling, Chubby walked back down to
the river feeling very unhappy.

"I'm not allowed to go in the water!" he told Mafuta.
"Then come and play in the mud!" said Mafuta.
"I'm not allowed to do that either!" said Chubby.
"Aren't you allowed to do anything?" asked Mafuta.
"I'm only allowed to roar," said Chubby miserably.
"We-ell, you're lucky," said Mafuta kindly, "I can't roar!"
"Nor can I…" Chubby sniffed and wiped a tear away with
one paw. "Not properly, I can't… my roar is too small…"

"Have you tried hard?" asked Mafuta. Chubby nodded.
"I've tried as hard as anything, but I can only roar a little
roar. I'll never, ever be able to roar a big, proper roar
like my papa… I know I won't ever…"
"You will Chubby," said Mafuta."
"I won't… I know I won't…"
said Chubby.

"Oh yes you will!" said Mafuta and pointed
to a deep cave in the rocks on the river-
bank. "Do you see that cave over there
Chubby? Well, that cave is full of echoes!
If you roar a little roar inside that cave, I
promise you, Chubby, it will sound like a
great, big roar!"
"Really?" said Chubby, "Are you sure?"
"Trust me." Said Mafuta, "I am as sure as
sure can be".
In a flash Chubby forgot all about the pool
and the mud pies and being cross! He did
two somersaults backwards with excitement
and raced across the veld, calling "Mama!
Mama! Papa! Papa! Come quickly! Come
and listen to me roar!"

"Well, then go ahead and roar" said Chubby's Mama, "and it had better be good, or you'll get it for waking us up again!"

"No, no! You have to follow me down to the big cave on the river bank!" shouted Chubby and ran off before they could say no.

"What is the naughty cub up to now?" grumbled Mama Lion but she and Papa Lion rose, stretched their limbs and followed through the grass with long slow strides. Down to the river bank they went and from there along to the cave in the rocks where Chubby was waiting, hopping about impatiently.

"Well?" growled Papa Lion, "Go ahead, roar!"

"Now you wait here and listen!" said Chubby and he ran into the cave by himself. It was dark inside, very dark, but Chubby didn't care. Right in the middle of the cave he stopped, took a deep breath and began to roar and roar and roar.

The sound of Chubby's little roars grew louder and louder, joined by all the echoes that started bouncing back and forth from the sides of the cave so that soon Chubby's little roars grew into a great, big, loud, rumbling, grumbling, growling ROARRRRRRR that shook the cave and the ground and the whole river bank!

When the very last sound of the big roar faded away
Chubby came trotting out of the cave. "Well, how was
that?" he asked. "Did you hear me roar?"
"Oh Chubby!" said Mama Lion, "That was one of the
best roars I've ever heard in my whole life!"
Papa Lion winked at Chubbby, "Wow Chubby," he said,
"What a roar! I am really proud of you!"
Very pleased, Chubby trotted off with his Mama and
Papa. Somehow he had the feeling that one day he
would know how to roar – how to roar properly, by
himself, without having to go into the cave.

THE END

More **African Tales** *to come:*

- Nyati, the Big Bad Buffalo

- Stranger in the Forest

- A New Coat for Bunny Boy

- Mafuta, the Baby Hippo

Made in the USA
Charleston, SC
20 June 2014